TIGER'S DEADLY SECRET

COMPANY 417 SHIFTERS SERIES

AMELIA WILSON

1

Maya

"Dr. Xavier?" Chirp asks. Her name isn't really Chirp. Damn it, I can't remember her name right now. She's my assistant for the last four years, for Pete's sake, starting as an intern in the summer before she starts college. Of course, nobody uses her real name, so it's not like I'm the only one.

Ah. I remember.

"What's up, Wilhelmina?"

Her eyes grow wide. "Oh no, am I in trouble?"

I laugh. "Do your parents use your first name?"

"Only when I'm in trouble," she says tentatively.

"When I was a kid, if Mom called, 'Maya!' I was fine. If Dad called, 'Celie!' I was fine. Man, if one of them called, "Maya Cecilia Xavier!' I was in deep doodoo."

A smile breaks out on her face. "Okay. I'm not in trouble. Why not Chirp, though?"

I laugh a little guiltily. "Because I forgot your name for a minute there."

She laughs and claps her hands. "That means we're finally friends. You know, every one of my friends ends up forgetting my name and trying to remember it. I've been Chirp for so long when I hear my actual name, it's always a business thing or a sales call." She winks and says, "Unless I'm in trouble."

"You're some perfect genius kid," I say, "What kind of trouble do you ever get in?"

She giggles and says, "Boy troubles." I chuckle at that and say, "Anyway, what did you need me for Doctor?"

"Did I call you a genius kid? I take that back. You're the one who started this conversation."

"Oh yeah! That subject, the last one, the last fireman guy, he just called. He can make the three o'clock appointment, but the new fire truck arrived so the maintenance he was scheduled to do on the old truck isn't happening so if it works better for you, he can arrive any time today."

I glance at the clock on the wall and then at my computer screen. It actually works out a whole lot better for me to get him in earlier. "How does an early day sound for you, Chirp?" I ask.

"As long as I'm Chirp getting off early and not Wilhelmina being sent home."

"Now I need to forget your name again. Go ahead and call him back. Tell him if he can show up at ten-thirty, that would be great. Then, while I finish up here, you go ahead and get the lab set up for me. Then, you can just enjoy your weekend if you like."

"Are you sure you don't need me to help?"

"He's the last guy and we've done nineteen already," I say, "So I'll be fine."

"Doctor, let me rephrase that," she says, "Are you sure I

can't watch the sexy fireman strip down to his boxer shorts?"

I chuckle and say, "You need to think about them as subjects and not sexy firemen."

"Yeah, right," she says, "Nobody is that scientific."

"You can stay if you want, Chirp," I say, "but no flirting."

She laughs and says, "I think maybe I better take the day off then. Actually, this helps. I have finals next week so I can use the extra study time. I'll get the lab ready."

Getting the lab ready is all that Chirp can do for me with this study. She thinks I'm measuring the impact of firefighting on the physiology of firefighters. It's not true at all. I mean, I'm studying that to an extent but for entirely different reasons.

I'm studying the impact of firefighting on shifter physiology as compared to human physiology. Chirp has no idea every one of the firefighters in this study is a shifter from a fire company of shifters.

Shifters are public now, or mostly public, but my family has been aware of shifters since before the community came out to the public. An ancestor of mine, also a doctor, saves a child from death in 1780. He discovers the child in the forest outside of Ontario, Canada, bleeding from a gunshot wound.

So Jericho Xavier takes the child back to the fort at Ontario and treats her. While he surgically removes the bullet, he notices differences in the child's physiology compared to the people he's operated on in the past, specifically in the strength of the child's muscle fibers and the elasticity of the connective tissue. We know now that those differences are related to the shifter ability to change size, shape, mass without harming themselves. He assumes that it's simply a difference in the physiology of the natives that live in the area until one day, the child shifts in the middle of an examination.

The child makes a full recovery, and because my ancestor realizes that others will immediately react in fear to the presence of a werewolf in their settlement, he takes the child back to the natives, who she says know her nature.

He returns to the natives, and what do you know, there's a whole tribe of wolf shifters—we don't call them werewolves anymore, although there's a population in Eastern Europe that still prefers the term lycanthrope.

Anyway, that's neither here nor there. Jericho Xavier discovers wolf shifters and therefore shifters in general and decides to help them, and ever since then, my family has provided medical research to the shifter community that they haven't been able or willing to find from the rest of the scientific world. In recent years, the Xavier Foundation has expanded from medical research to numerous other scientific fields, all specifically related to shifters.

It's easy enough to disguise our true purpose from the rest of the world. We call ourselves a normal scientific think tank and justify the heightened level of secrecy by telling people that our research is highly sensitive and we don't want a for-profit company—we're supported entirely by our family's considerable successful financial investments over the past two hundred forty plus years—to steal our research and use it for gain, which is completely true.

So now you understand why I—a non-shifter—am about to perform a medical examination on a shifter. It's not something he would likely trust anyone else to do, but I'm a Xavier, and shifters know my family.

My shifter arrives, and he is hot as hell. I don't just mean typical, oh, he's a firefighter, he's hot, I mean, oh, he's the sexiest creature to ever walk on God's green earth and if there was any way on Earth I could convince him to have sex with me without it being utterly inappropriate, I would be naked and gripping his ass to pull his cock deeper into me as we speak.

He smiles and shakes my hand and says, “Good morning, Doctor. I’m Owen Avery.” When he does, I almost decide to hell with appropriateness, I’m getting laid.

But--*sigh*--I’m a professional, so instead, I only say, “It’s nice to meet you. I’m Doctor Maya Xavier.”

“A beautiful name,” he says, and his voice is every bit as sexy as his toned, powerful body.

I somehow manage to keep from moaning as I ask him to strip, and when he does, I am glad that I send Chirp home early because she would absolutely be able to tell that I’m attracted to Owen.

2

Owen

Despite my misgivings about this study, I can't deny that the sight of Doctor Xavier is a very nice sight to behold. I don't know how a girl can be so attractive while wearing a lab coat. I mean, it pretty much covers up her form but not enough to hide that her body is extraordinary. I know it makes me an asshole to be so focused on her appearance and her body. I can't help it, though. I'm a remnant of a prior world, I guess.

I suppose also, part of the focus on her body has to do with how much of mine is exposed. I'm wearing only my boxer shorts at the moment. From what Garrett and Micah tell me from their appointments, they'll come off at some point near the end of the investigation as well. I know this is clinical and not amorous, but I can't pretend not to want this woman.

Another thing working against me when it comes to

restraint is that this woman already knows I'm a shifter. She's Franklin Xavier's granddaughter and the Xavier family knows about us long before we go public to the world. This study is specific to shifters although this aspect of the study is secret. Shifters experience far fewer of the ailments typical to firefighter than non-shifters. This is across the board, meaning wolf shifters, horse shifters, or any other shifters all remain far less likely to be hurt in the course of duty. That might be attributed to the generally better physiques we possess but we're also less likely to have chronic illness from exposure to chemicals and smoke.

Dr. Xavier hopes to discover if the phenomenon has to do with our physiology or if we perform our duties differently than non-shifters in ways we don't necessarily realize. If it's our physiology, the goal will likely to be recruitment of more shifters. If we do things differently, there will be recommended courses of action for non-shifters to better firefighter health and safety.

I draw in breath sharply and Dr. Xavier says, "Sorry. I know the stethoscope can be cold."

"No problem," I say. "Just startled me." Of course, I'm lying through my teeth. I drew in breath because her free hand brushed against my abdomen briefly just as she set the stethoscope down and a jolt of electricity seems to run through me when it does.

"You're a tiger, right?" she asks.

"Yes, Ma'am," I lie. Well, it's not really a lie. It just isn't the full truth.

"I have to tell you, you may be the healthiest tiger I've ever met," she says.

"Really?"

She removes the stethoscope and says, "Your resting heart rate is very slow and measured. That's something that only comes with very good health. Ultimately, by the time you're old, your heart will have beat only about seventy percent as many times as most tigers and a third as many times as most pure humans. Unless something really unforeseen happens, you're not going to die from any kind of cardiac problems."

"You're saying I have a lot of heart?"

She chuckles and says, "You have a special heart, I guess." She blushes and it makes me want her more.

Actually, it makes me decide I will have her. It's not the tiger in me that makes that decision. In general, the tiger in me is far less rational and careful than what makes the decision. The tiger in me doesn't just run amok. The tiger in me has more restraint when it comes to interacting with female perfection. The tiger in me doesn't make the decision. What makes the decision is the other part of me.

The secret part.

The dragon.

"Lift your arm, please," she says.

I comply and she presses the stethoscope to a spot on my side just in front of where my wings sprout when I shift to my dragon form, although in human form there's nothing that could tell her that I'm a dragon, regardless of how long she examines me or how sophisticated her equipment.

That's a good thing.

See, shifters aren't supposed to have two animals. As far as I know, I'm the only one alive. Many shifter couples are interspecies. Plenty of wolves marry tigers and plenty of bears marry stags. Well, the second one is less common since carnivores don't typically marry herbivores, but it happens. It's not something anyone would turn their heads at, and the worst you can expect is an unintentionally insensitive ribbing from family members.

They have kids too. Here's the thing, though: those kids are always one animal *or* the other, not both. What I mean is, a child of a tiger and a wolf might be either a tiger or a wolf, but never both. There's always one human form and one animal form.

Unless you're half dragon.

Dragons are to shifters what the rest of the shifter community is to humans. It's generally understood that we exist, but it's not common knowledge how many of us exist and most shifters have never seen one. We don't come out with the rest of the shifter community because while humans for the most part can accept the existence of humans who turn into animals, humans who turn into exceptionally strong and powerful mythical creatures are much harder to stomach.

So not much is known about us even among shifters, and we like to keep it that way. You know those old legends about knights who slay dragons? Well, we'd like to avoid that, if possible.

Anyway, dragons rarely marry. They rarely have sex too. When they do, they take steps to ensure that sex won't result in children. And they never mate with other shifters.

The reasons for this are essentially the same as the reasons we keep our nature secret to begin with, with one important exception: it's much harder to avoid having children when we mate with shifters than when we mate with ordinary humans. Don't ask me why, I don't know. I only know that when my father falls in love with my mother, he knows that doing so means having a child. Having a child in the dragon community is much more serious than the normal shifter community. All shifters are long-lived, but dragons are far longer-lived than other shifters. If we have too many kids, then we will soon run out of the ability to keep ourselves secret, not to mention we'll control more of the wealth in the world than we already do, and we already control a considerable amount of that.

Maya pulls me from my thoughts by sticking her hand down my boxers and gently grasping my balls. My eyes widen in shock until she says, "Turn your head and cough for me."

I somehow manage to keep from getting an erection as I comply, and it's among the hardest things I've ever done in my life.

I want her. I will have her. She is mine.

I can't have her now because I start a four-day shift in an hour, but I will be back here to claim what belongs to me when that shift is over.

3

Maya

You would imagine the Xavier family has a great many shifter/human pairings given our centuries-long relationship with shifters. The truth is, we don't have all that many in our history. This is because part of what makes our relationship work is that we serve as a sort of secret liaison to the world of humans. Oddly, since shifters went public, that work is even more difficult than before. The truth is, there are probably more people now that adamantly refuse to believe in shifters than before they announced themselves to the world.

A shifter relationship isn't off limits or anything. It just doesn't usually happen for a Xavier. It's not forbidden fruit. It's not even explicitly frowned upon. If I need to pick a word to describe it, I think maybe I'll choose unfashionable. That's it. It might be seen as something garish, not disrespectful exactly but almost putting a foot into the world we're supposed to protect instead of protecting that world with all our hearts.

So, maybe there's a bit of naughtiness that flavors things for me as my fingertips lightly move over my skin and I think about Firefighter Owen Avery. I can say right now that it isn't just his body making me feel this way. All shifters, in general, have human physiques that are more well-defined and attractive than pure humans. As far as attributes below the belt, the truth is there's as much variety in shifters as in humans.

And Owen Avery has very, very impressive attributes.

But I'm serious. It isn't his physical makeup that turns me on. It certainly doesn't hurt but what drives these feelings for the most part have a whole hell of a lot more to do with the man's personality. He has a bearing that's... How can I explain it? All tiger shifters display a kind of regality. It's innate. You might expect that to be more pronounced with lions but the whole King of the Jungle thing is a human invention. Lion shifters appear catlike in their movements, lithe and balanced, almost sleek. The same goes for jaguars, panthers, and leopards. Tigers have that but there is a definitely regal aspect to their bearing that supersedes the rest.

I don't mean they appear arrogant. To me, the humblest thing possible is sheer power not displayed. The humblest thing possible is regality with an unassuming nature. Those contradictions are very prevalent in Tiger shifters.

But there's more.

This an almost aloof fascination with the world around him. I know aloof and fascination appear incompatible, like you can't be both aloof and fascinated. I get that. I can't explain it other than it almost seems like he's seen everything possible there is to see but always keeps his eyes open for what new curiosity he might discover.

Yeah... Maybe I'm just thinking about how he has a very big dick. I mean, as my fingers trail over my breasts and I feel the need growing between my legs, I can't claim that I'm having an easy time focusing on his personality anymore.

My hands slide over my body, everywhere but the one place I desperately want to feel them, or rather the place I want to feel him. I close my eyes and imagine Owen's hands traveling over me with that incredible restrained power he shows.

So that's another thing about him that I find fascinating. Power under restraint. That's not a medical term or a philosophical term, at least that I'm aware of. It's just the best way I can think of to describe the fact that Owen is clearly incredibly dangerous but keeps that danger in check. It's like... think of a famous martial artist or maybe a strongman. That person is probably incredibly dangerous if he or she wanted to be. Not to put too fine a point on it, but a professional strongman would probably very easily be able to hurt or kill someone, but they don't. In fact, they manage to be in many cases even more soft-handed and gentle than other people, because the consequences of losing control in their case is far more serious than in the case of an average person.

A lot of shifters show power under restraint. Nearly all of them in fact. They have to. Even a smaller shifter, like an ocelot or a bobcat shifter is far more dangerous than even the most dangerous non-shifter martial artists or strongmen. See, shifters in animal form are for reasons we still don't understand anywhere from three to five times larger than their animal counterparts, but they're not three to five times stronger. They're more like five to eight times stronger. That means a bobcat shifter could weigh up to two hundred pounds in animal form and will be significantly stronger than a human athlete of the same weight. A tiger shifter might way up to eleven hundred pounds and be strong enough to take down a bull elephant.

That's another thing that's sexy as hell, not that Owen is dangerous, but that I feel perfectly safe with him even knowing he's dangerous. That and I know that it takes a lot of effort for him to keep from literally fucking me to death, and when he finally releases just a fraction of the power, he's going to fuck me so hard and so thoroughly that I'm probably going to spend the rest of that day and most of the next just trembling in bed from the force of my multiple orgasms.

God, I wish he was here right now. I have an active imagination, but it's not enough to truly comprehend what it would feel like to have his cock inside me.

Well, it'll have to do.

I slide my fingers into my pussy, and when I do, I gasp and shake and despite my modest abilities compared to those I imagine Owen has, I nearly cum the moment my fingers travel over my g-spot. When I slide my other hand down to stroke my clit while I finger myself, I nearly cum again, and this time, the pleasure doesn't recede but hovers right on the edge.

"Oh God, Owen," I say, "Oh God, yes. I'm yours. I'm yours."

It's not normal for me to fantasize about being so submissive. I'm more the kind of girl who likes to be on top, if you know what I mean.

Not with Owen. That man can do whatever he wants to me, however he wants to me, whenever he wants to me on command, and the only concern I will have is will I remain conscious or will the force of the orgasms knock me out.

"Owen!" I cry out as the orgasm I give myself hits me like a tidal wave.

I shriek and jerk and writhe on the bed, moaning and gasping and shuddering, and while I'm sure Owen could do a better job were he here to do it, I still manage to make myself cum harder than I ever have in my life.

4

Owen

Today is not thirty years ago. Thirty years ago, the idea of actively pursuing a Xavier is likely absurd. The family is, in some ways, the most important family for shifters in the last two-hundred and fifty years or so. They opened up avenues to allow shifters access to the changing world. There were doctor shifters prior to Jericho Xavier but very few. There were far more shamans and charlatans than actual doctors, too.

In general, shifters heal much faster than humans. The process of shifting speeds healing as well so a bear gravely injured in human form can shift into a bear who will be seriously injured instead of gravely injured. A shift back an hour later, and he's badly injured. The point is, medical needs for shifters are different than medical needs for humans. Perhaps the most difficult to address are injuries or illnesses obtained in animal form. Human doctors can't fathom how they happened and so prior to shifter physicians becoming more available, real care isn't possible.

Jericho Xavier's legacy is a foundation that changes that. Not only have most shifter physicians attended medical school because of Xavier scholarships but they also attend special seminars designed for shifter care.

The point is, the Xavier's are the most respected humans on Earth. Most bears will respect a Xavier descendant more than a wolf. The wolves will respect and Xavier more than a bear. Yeah, in the shifter world, there are prejudices and preferences like in the human world. Of course, shifters are correct about their prejudices in relation to other shifters. Incompatibilities animal to animal don't disappear when the animal has a human form. No matter how close a horse shifter gets to a wolf shifter or another predator, there is always an element of distrust that can't be altered, which is why marriages between carnivores and herbivores, while not unheard of, are uncommon.

I think my Dragon nature makes me rise above all that. I don't dislike panthers because of their hyperactivity or lions because of their gregarious nature. I don't dislike wolves for being such damned drama queens and I don't dislike bears for being such stereotypical forest rangers. I don't dislike horses for being skittish. I rise above all that.

Before you go thinking I mean that as a compliment, I don't. I rise above it because dragons are inherently superior to all other creatures.

Yeah, what an ego, right?

I can't help that, though. It's a physiological thing for me to feel this way. The truth is, I'll live two or three times longer than my firefighter brothers. Maybe. I say maybe because we don't know for sure. My father will most definitely live for seven-hundred years. He may live twice that long. We don't know for sure because there are no longer any natural dragons on Earth, but the general theory is that natural dragons could not die by natural causes but would live forever absent a violent death or an external illness. Who knows.

But I am half dragon and half tiger. So, my parents theorize a substantial lifespan but not as long as my father's.

Let me get back to the Xavier family. They are great friends to all shifter kind. In fact, two-hundred years ago, dragons revealed themselves to the Xavier family. It took them ten thousand years to reveal themselves to other shifters, but Jericho Xavier and his foundation represent pure, unadulterated good. So, aspiring to be with a Xavier daughter is almost unthinkable.

But I will have her.

Dr. Maya Xavier will be mine.

"Will you pay attention, please, Shere Khan?" Lucas says from across the yard.

"Oh leave him alone," Garret replies, "Heeeee's Grrrrreat!"

I chuckle. "I feel so threatened when an overgrown kitten and a monkey tease me."

"Hey!" Garret says in mock anger. "Apes aren't monkeys!"

"Ahem, fine tiger who isn't in any way fallible," Lucas says, "Can you please turn on the water now?"

"Of course, lesser being," I say.

Lucas rolls his eyes and says, "I might be smaller than you, Owen, but think about the level of my mouth and your nuts the next time you—"

He stops and reddens, realizing what he's about to say. I smile placidly at him while Garret does a very poor job of hiding laughter. "Just turn on the fucking water," Lucas says, grinning sheepishly and shaking his head.

"Anything for you, sugarlips," I say.

"Seriously," Garret chokes out, "Why would you say that, Lucas?"

"Why, are you jealous?" Lucas asks.

I turn the water on, and Garret examines the hose for leaks while saying, "Yeah, there's no coming back from that, Lucas. You're fucked."

"Well, keep in mind, leopards eat gorillas in the wild," Lucas says.

Garret grins at him, and a moment later, Lucas reddens further and says, "Oh, fuck you!"

"Yeah," I say, "You might want to stop talking, Lucas."

"Oh whatever," he says, "Suck a dick, Owen."

"If I ever do, I know who to call for tips and tricks," I retort.

"Both of you shut up," Garret says, "I don't want to have a hardon in front of the captain."

"Is he coming in today?" Lucas asks.

"Yep," Garret says, "Inspection. Why do you think we're checking the hoses for leaks less than a week after we checked them before? You can shut the water off now, Owen."

I close the spigot and Lucas begins wrapping up the hose. "What time is the captain coming in?" I ask.

"Gonna ask for some time off?" Lucas asks with a grin.

It's an inside joke. I'm one of a few firefighters here who rarely, if ever, take time off. The other firefighters who enjoy a more normal vacation schedule tease us for being workaholics, but we don't mind.

Today is different though.

"Actually," I say, "I am."

Both Garret and Lucas look up in surprise. Garret figures it out first. He grins and says, "So, his Royal Majesty has finally found a girlfriend."

"Seriously?" Lucas says, "That's fucked up, bro. I thought what we had was special."

"I'll always treasure the time we had," I tell him, "But it's time we both moved on."

Before Lucas can make a retort, an alarm goes off. Then another. Then another. When the fourth alarm goes off, any pretext at humor is gone.

We exchange a look, then rush to the lockers to gear up. A four-alarm fire doesn't necessarily mean that four teams need to respond, but it does mean the fire is very serious and the threat of spreading and loss of life is very high.

We're dressed and in the engine in less than five minutes and as the engine peels from the station and accelerates down the road, sirens blaring, I hear Garret say, "Oh fuck."

"What is it?" I ask.

"It's a Xavier business," he says, "The fire."

My blood runs cold. The only Xavier business within our area of responsibility is Maya's lab.

"How soon will we get there?" I ask.

"Eleven minutes," Lucas replies from the cab.

"Let's make it eight," I say.

There's no protest from Lucas. Everyone knows how important the Xaviers are. He accelerates faster and when I see the smoke in the distance, I can only hope we're not already too late.

5

Maya

So, this is how I die.

I feel strangely calm under the circumstances.

You know, I haven't lived very long. I'm twenty-seven years old. Maybe that's why I don't have any regrets. Maybe I would be more upset about my death with regrets. Maybe regrets make people more panicked when it happens.

Jesus. I'm in shock.

I'm not strangely calm, I'm responding to the situation with near paralysis instead of action.

No, I'm slipping into shock. I'm not there, yet. If I were, thoughts like this won't come to mind. It takes a great deal of effort to lift up my hand and whack myself across the face. I manage it, though, and immediately shout, "Funky butt lovin'!" Yeah, I saw it in a baseball movie for kids when a doctor got his nose broken. Now it's my standard response to pain. If you want to judge me, go ahead, now's the time. I'm not really in a position to make up some kind of snappy comeback at the moment.

But the blow does the trick, and my flight or fight survival mode comes back. I look at Chirp. She's on the ground because of a tank explosion. The CO2 is used to power some pneumatic equipment. The explosion, thankfully, didn't send shrapnel flying through the air. The tank ruptured and split. Maybe that's a safety feature.

The point is that a piece of the tank crashed into a cabinet which broke off the wall and hit Chirp. She's breathing. She's also on the ground, safest from the smoke. I slide to the ground and crawl over to her. She's unconscious but there are no visible signs of injury. Her breathing is regular. I check her pulse. Typical sleeping pulse. She's just knocked out. There may be a concussion to deal with but she's stable for now.

This lab is state of the art. The actual chances of a fire are extraordinarily small. The chances of fire occurring and the suppression system not working are even smaller. Frankly, I'm unprepared. Jesus, I know we have an emergency exit plan, but even though it's posted via a little plaque in every single damned room, I don't have any idea what it's supposed to be. I mean, who looks at that? These things aren't supposed to happen.

Flames cover the front wall as well as the wall to the room through which I might go escape via the back door. I'm not going to make it out of the lab on my own, so the only thing I can do is find a way to buy myself more time until the sprinklers come on or until fire and rescue arrive to pull me out. There are no windows large enough to crawl through from any of the rooms and even if I do, I have no idea if any of the doors are safe to open. The fire didn't start right here. Who the hell knows where it starts, actually? While I'm thinking about things who the hell knows, *how* the hell am I supposed to buy myself time until the cavalry arrives?

Remaining close to the ground is a critical, of course. I can't just leave Chirp here, either.

I look around, hoping that an idea will miraculously present itself while I stare around the room. What an excellent strategy. Why do people do this? I mean, what, is a floating lightbulb supposed to pop up when we look around and miraculously provide the solution to the problem?

There's no floating lightbulb, but I'll take the oxygen masks that pop up. Those will be just fine.

Okay, they don't actually pop up. I see them in a drawer labeled OXYGEN MASKS AND MISC. BREATHING EQUIP.

I crawl over and grab two, then crawl back to Chirp. The air is hazy with smoke, and I'm already gasping for breath from the heat and the rapidly lowering oxygen levels in the room.

I put my mask on first, remembering the rule they tell you on airplanes to put your own mask on first before helping others. That rule seems self-serving on the surface, but when you think about it, you can't help anyone if you're unconscious, and I nearly am when I finally manage to get the mask on and pull the cord releasing the oxygen.

I put Chirp's mask on and am relieved when I see the respirator start to fog and know that she's still breathing.

Now I need to find a way out of here, and fast. The heat from the fire is impossible—searing and debilitating. It has to be close to two hundred degrees in here, but it's not the heat that will kill us. These masks have maybe five minutes of internal oxygen without hooking them up to the building's oxygen supply, which I can't do because while the masks do a decent job of insulating against heat, if there's so much as a pinhole leak in the oxygen hoses, well, if you want to know what happens when oxygen meets fire, look up a NASA space shuttle launch. From what I understand, the main component of liquid rocket fuel is oxygen.

We don't have time. We just don't have time.

I try the door to the room I know I can't escape from, and it's searing hot. I try the door to the room we're in, knowing I can't leave through there either, and it's searing hot. I don't try the window because the window is engulfed in flames, and anyway, if I open it, the difference in pressure will cause the room to explode in flames like a bomb.

We're going to die here.

Now the panic starts to set in. I'm not sure if panic is better than shock, but it doesn't matter. I could be perfectly calm and content right now; I'll be just as dead in a few minutes.

God, it's so hot.

I try to focus, but all I end up doing is just looking at the same exits I already know I can't use and getting more and more panicked as time goes on.

Then salvation arrives in the form of the goddamned Fire Authority. All firefighters are sexy, but when I see the Company 417 patch on their uniforms, they're the sexiest creatures who've ever lived.

We're going to be okay.

They breach the room and one of them immediately picks Chirp up and carries her toward the exit. I get slowly to my feet, and one of the other firefighters asks me, "Can you walk?"

His voice sounds familiar, but as my panic recedes, shock sets in, and I'm not able to place it. "Yes," I say, "I can walk."

Then my vision swims and the last thing I'm aware of before I pass out is my legs buckling as the firefighter catches me and picks me up off of the ground. I go in and out of consciousness as we exit the building. When I come to, I'm sitting on the curb in the parking lot, and staring up at the face of my now maskless rescuer.

"Owen," I whisper.

"It's okay," he says, "You're safe now."

6

Owen

This woman saved her assistant's life. She saved her own life as well. The medical oxygen tanks, intended for emergencies and not for extended use, are the only thing that keeps them alive. Hell, they're really not worse for wear at all. The assistant, Wilhelmina Gardener, has a slight concussion. Maya is fine. It's only the urging of four different firemen that gets Doctor Marvin to insist she stay overnight for observation. Marvin doesn't take much convincing, actually. He's not a shifter but he owes his education to the Xavier foundation and knows the reality behind the firefighters pushing him.

Maya isn't happy about it, but Wilhelmina says if Maya doesn't stay overnight, she's not staying either. I like that girl, she's plucky. Do people still use that term, *plucky*? While Wilhelmina is distracted, I whisper in Maya's ear, "Does she know?"

Maya whispers back, "No."

God. It's fucking stupid of me to be so excited about the closeness and the whispering, especially when it's about something entirely nonromantic. Still, my mind responds the way it does. "Any news on what caused the fire?" Wilhelmina asks.

"There's no chance of finding that out until tomorrow," I say. At the moment, we're in the emergency room. A curtain could separate the two of them, but it doesn't at the moment. I'll be here until they're brought up to their overnight rooms. "And it may take days past that, depending on the cause and how much damage we have to sift through."

"All the research," Wilhelmina groans.

"No, Chirp," Maya says, "Everything is backed up to cloud after every shift. It's already in New Haven and even if it weren't, we can get it." She means New Haven, Connecticut, where the Xavier Foundation is based.

"So now, we just need a new lab."

Maya nods and says in a voice that doesn't sound nearly as calm and as happy as the words, "We can afford it." It may just be the shock of the fire, but I hear something in her voice that tells me she's troubled. None of her behavior since getting to the hospital suggests any emotional shock is affecting her. Of course, I may just be inordinately interested in her and seeking to believe I understand her better than I do. I'm willing to admit that's another thing I get from my dragon nature. It's hard to think things are all that complicated when you're essentially a living and breathing weapon of mass destruction. It's hard to think you don't know everything when you have a lifespan that gives you a great deal more wisdom than most creatures.

If not for Wilhelmina, I might… Wait a minute. "Did you call her Chirp?"

Wilhelmina laughs. "That's my nickname. Everyone calls me that. Ever since I was a baby."

"Why did you get that nickname?"

"Not even hunky fireman who save my life get that information, pal."

I laugh but then Maya says, "Sorry, Chirp. Firefighter Avery saved my life. It was another hunky fireman who saved you."

Chirp says, "Well, then, you're definitely not getting the story about my nickname."

I feel like a complete fool for feeling happy about the slight touch of jealousy in Maya's voice when she points out that I'm the hunky firefighter who saves her life, but that's how I feel. The dragon in my nature wonders why I should feel like a fool for enjoying the fact that the woman who belongs to me should be possessive of me, but right now, the human nature is winning out.

Fortunately, the firefighter wins out over both natures, and although both the dragon and the human—and the tiger for that matter—would rather stay with Maya, I manage to find the strength to leave after their rooms are assigned. I do promise to check up on both of them in the morning and feel another rush of foolish joy when I see the quick jealous glance Maya shoots Chirp's way.

She has nothing to worry about. She's the one who belongs to me, and anyway, Chirp may notice I'm attractive, but Lucas gets the longer and more meaningful glances from her.

I head back to the station and see if I can find any information that might help us learn what started the fire. At the moment, there's no information other than what we've gleaned from the scene, which isn't much. Shortly after we evacuate the lab, an oxygen leak causes the fire to burn exceptionally hot. We manage to turn the oxygen off quickly so we avoid an explosion, but there's nothing left of the lab to indicate a cause.

Rather than sleeping soundly as I normally do after a long shift, I lay awake for much of the night thinking of Maya. I stare at the bunk above me, but my eyes are filled with images of Maya in her lab coat and quite a few fantasized images of her out of her lab coat.

I must have her. I will have her. She is mine.

I manage to get some sleep, because it's my alarm that wakes me, unusual but not unheard of for me. I roll out of bed, shower and dress in less than an hour. I check out of the station and head immediately to the hospital.

When I arrive at the hospital, Maya is sitting up in her room and talking. I confer briefly with Marvin, who tells me she has a clean bill of health and will be sent home in a couple of hours barring a disaster.

She smiles when I walk inside, and I ask, "Hi. How are you doing?"

"Well, I've been better," she says.

I chuckle and say, "Yes, I'm so sorry about your lab."

She flips her hand. "I'm sure I'll have a new one within the week. The foundation has a lot of money and a lot of friends, as you know."

I do know. When the dragons reveal themselves to the Xaviers, they essentially guarantee that the Xaviers have access to unlimited wealth. Not that Maya knows that I'm a dragon or even exactly where her family's wealth comes from.

"Any news?" she asks, "On what caused this?"

I shake my head. "I don't suppose you have any ideas."

It's her turn to shake her head. "That lab is—was—beyond state of the art. The Air Force could have launched an assault on us, and the lab wouldn't have gone up in flames like that. It has to be some kind of arson."

"That's a very serious accusation," I say.

"It has to be," she says. "There was no reason for the sprinklers not to work."

We are interrupted by Marvin, who smiles and informs Maya that she can stay the final two hours of her twelve-hour observation window, or she can go home.

"No offense, Doctor," she says, "But the sooner I'm out of here, the better."

Twenty minutes later, I drop her off at home. Two seconds after the door closes behind us, her lips are on mine.

7

Maya

My brain never really shuts off. So, as much as I want to focus on the moment, I can't dismiss the very obvious reality that my behavior is in part driven by the threat of death averted. I don't mean I'm going to sleep with this man because I'm grateful. Well, I'm certain gratitude plays into all the reasons I'm attracted to him, of course, but it isn't the primary driving force. Ordinarily, no level of attraction is going to make me act spur of the moment.

I'm a doctor and a scientist, for Pete's sake.

Well, this medical research scientist is kissing Owen more passionately than she's ever kissed anyone before. My mind may be narrating reasons and thoughts all through the process but that doesn't change a damned thing. Regardless of the reason for my behavior, this is going to happen, and any regret that might come from that, I'll save for later.

Owen's hands move over my body. I'm sure it's the excitement of the situation and simply the attraction I feel for him but it sure as hell feels like this man does more with his hands through my clothing than any man has been able to do for me when I'm fully clothed.

Fully clothed.

The thought gets my own hands moving and I must admit that as I work my way down his button-down shirt, more than one button is too frustrating and just ends up falling to the floor when I pull the shirt apart. I guess me undressing him gives Owen permission because I have to stop what I'm doing as my arms come up and he pulls my shirt over my head.

From there, any plans to undress each other disappear. We both start tearing at our own clothes. I'm pretty sure the bra I wear will need a new catch. I don't give a damn. I get my bra off, kick off my shoes, get my pants down, and slide my panties down. I get them to my knees before suddenly I'm in the air because Owen lifts me up. I have to grab onto his shoulder to keep from falling backward. Since I'm there, though, I kiss him again.

He moves through my house, kicking open doors. I could tell him where my bedroom is, of course, but this is so damned sexy, I want it to continue. So, I hold him and kiss him until he steps into a room and tosses me on the bed. It's not my bedroom. It's the guest room. Who cares, right?

He still wears his boxers. Seeing the cotton strain against his very obvious and very large erection is damned exciting. I kick my legs to get my panties down to my ankles and then manage to get them off. By then, he's naked and approaching. For the first time, I feel kind of paralyzed. It isn't terror, not exactly. Let me just say that his cock is damned intimidating.

I figure on starting with my mouth while I work up the courage for the rest of it, but he has other plans, and I gasp as he grabs my ankles and swings me so my ass is right on the edge of the mattress. I'm probably wetter than I've ever been in my life, but that doesn't make the thought of that cock thrusting into me like this is pretty damned scary.

That's not his plan.

Abruptly, he falls to his knees. That puts his face right in front of my pussy, but it still shocks me when his mouth gets there.

This isn't the first time I have oral sex, but it's the first time I have sex of any kind with someone as attractive as Owen. Maybe it's just arrogance that leads me to believe that oral sex is something you give to someone because they're more attractive than you, and you want to convince them to let you have intercourse with them or because you want a girl to suck your cock and you think if you eat them out, they'll have to reciprocate.

So I don't expect Owen to eat my pussy because he's so fucking hot he can have my mouth no matter what, and he definitely doesn't have to convince me to fuck him. When his lips close over my pussy, I'm so surprised that I don't even have the wherewithal to form any words. All I can do is gasp and shudder and twitch as his lips and tongue work miracles in between my legs.

Seriously, it's like he was born to do this. He explores all of my folds, stimulating nerves I don't even know I have before now, and his tongue flicks rapidly over my clit with the perfect balance of speed and pressure.

When I cum, I *cum*. The orgasm I give myself two nights ago with my fingers is absolutely nothing compared to the earth-shattering explosion of pleasure that courses through me like a series of tsunamis, overwhelming me and filling me with sensations so powerful it's a wonder I even remain conscious.

When I can finally draw in breath, I prepare to cry out, "Owen, yes!" but the words die on my lips when he suddenly lifts himself and fills me with exactly what I never knew I needed. When his cock opens me and stretches me out more than I've ever been stretched in my life, the orgasm seems to come from somewhere deep inside me and radiates outward with powerful, agonizing pulses that merge with the electric shocks radiating from my clit and intensify everything I feel until I think I might actually die from the force of it.

Not a bad way to go.

"Owen!" I finally manage to shriek after two-and-a-half minutes of solid, intense climax. "Oh God, Owen!"

To say this is the best sex of my life would be like saying that caviar and venison is better than instant noodles. There's nothing wrong with instant noodles, and there's nothing wrong with average sex. If there was, then a whole lot of men and more women than we care to admit would be out of luck.

But if you have a choice between a foam cup of freeze dried soup and a five-star dinner of venison and caviar, what are you going to choose?

"God, Owen!" I cry out as my third orgasm hits me.

This one is even more powerful than the previous two combined because apparently turning my entire pussy into a solid, throbbing mass of achingly satisfied nerve endings isn't enough and he decides he has to massage my clit with one hand and use the other to softly squeeze my throat while he fucks me.

Remember I told you about restrained power? Well, it turns me on a *whole* lot. I cum so hard for so long, that I'm still shuddering and gasping when Owen cries out and I feel his cum spurt deep into me, and my teeth still chatter when I rest my head on his chest and fall to a deep, satisfying sleep.

8

Owen

I open my door and I'm not as delighted to see Maya as I ordinarily am. After three weeks and nearly every free moment spent with her, my infatuation with her is past it's egotistically-driven possessive stage. That has nothing to do with why I'm not delighted. It's only the news I have to share that makes me feel this way. Without the news, there is nothing buy joy at the sight of her.

"What's wrong?" she asks.

Dragons are essentially unreadable. We don't display emotions the way others do. To an extent, my dragon nature is modified by my tiger nature but not that aspect of my dragon nature. The exceptions to being unreadable exist only in three ways. First, dragons can read dragons. Second, mothers of dragons can read their children. My mother, the only nonhuman dragon mother in existence can read my emotions. All of the other dragon mothers are human, at least the ones still alive. Like I said, it's generally believed that all full dragons have died out.

The third exception is a woman a dragon loves.

So, her knowing anything is wrong tells me my feelings for her are deep, very deep.

"Your suspicions are right. It was arson. In addition, the sprinkler system was compromised mechanically. Someone actually filled the feeding pipe with lead."

"I knew it. That building was too safe for that to happen without intention." She sighs and steps in. I close the door behind her and turn around. "But why?" she asks. "The lab had no signage, so nobody could have known it was an Xavier Foundation lab. Even if they did, we're not a famous foundation. If you're not a doctor, you've never heard of us. If you're not a shifter, we're just a philanthropic institution that funds medical training and research."

"Anyone who delivered equipment or supplies would see the name on the invoice," I say.

She shakes her head. "No. It all goes to City Side Laboratories. We don't advertise the connection. I mean anywhere. We don't have it on any websites, and we don't have it... My parents. They specifically don't want my lab traceable."

"Why not?"

She shrugs. "Because I'm an heiress. I mean, my family has more than a hundred million dollars. The foundation is close to a billion right now, but we have a great deal of personal wealth, too. We certainly don't advertise that but if my parents had their way, I would live in a mansion with a gate and guards and not in the suburb."

I don't tell her this, but the foundation has access to close to a trillion dollars in wealth, even if the vast majority of that wealth isn't officially theirs. You might think that kind of wealth is intimidating. It's not. Add up the fortunes of the five wealthiest men on Earth. There are twenty different dragons with more than their combined wealth. Live for centuries and that happens. Also, the stories about dragons hoarding their treasure is true. Sure, we hoard stocks and securities more than gold and gems now, but the hoarding still happens. The tiger in me is far more free-spirited in that regard. My mother thinks I'm a tightwad miser. My father thinks I'm an irresponsible spendthrift.

The point is the money she talks about doesn't intimidate me. It does, however, make me look at the situation in a new light. "We need to stop thinking about this as something involving the Xavier Foundation and start looking at who gains from hurting you."

"I'm an only child. There are no other heirs and if I die before my parents, all of the money goes to various charities, none getting as much as a million dollars," she says, "So there aren't any jealous relatives waiting in the wings, if that's what you're suggesting."

I gesture to the couch, the couch where I hoped to soon be making love to Maya if I hadn't received the news I just relate to her.

"What if your parents were killed too?" I ask.

She looks at me in alarm, and I explain, "I'm sorry to bring that up, but we have to consider it. Could someone stand to benefit if both you and your parents were killed?"

"No," she says, "The language of their wills is ironclad. It's been that way for generations. Before an heir or heiress can succeed, they need to write a will leaving everything they own to one successor and one successor only. If something happens to that successor, then the wealth is liquidated. My ancestors did this specifically to prevent a situation like the kind you're talking about."

"Wise of them," I say. "Well then perhaps the motive isn't money. Could anyone be interested in hurting you personally?"

"No," she says. "I don't mean to brag, but I get along with everyone."

"There's not a rival who might be jealous of your success as a medical researcher?"

She shakes her head. "Unless they work directly with shifters too, they probably don't know who I am. That's also intentional, for obvious reasons."

I know what she means. It wouldn't do for the leading foundation of shifter medical research to occupy a prominent place in the medical world. Shifters are still very secretive, and considering the sensitive nature of the Foundation's work, they have to work extra hard to be relatively unknown.

"Someone from your personal life?" I ask, "An ex-lover, maybe?"

She laughs. "Unless you've suddenly developed a desire to hurt me, my last lover is Roger Waterston from college."

"Love lost leaves a deep wound," I say.

Her eyebrow lifts. "Well look at you. Hot and poetic."

I smile and say, "Just another of my many talents."

She giggles and her voice is sultry when she says, "You are certainly very talented."

Perhaps I'll get to make love to her after all. Not yet, though. The business of this arson is more important.

"How did Roger react when you broke up with him?" I ask.

She chuckles again. "Actually, he broke up with me."

I stare at her in shock. Very few things shock me, but the idea that someone could have Maya Xavier and choose to let her go is one of them. She laughs when she sees my face and says, "Like you say, love lost leaves a deep wound.

Roger had a high school sweetheart, Mary-Louise, and even when we were together, he would talk wistfully of how much he loved her. When she showed up at the same grad school as the two of us, we were history."

"Was she jealous when she heard of you two?" I ask.

She smiles, "Hard to be jealous when the guy dumps his girlfriend and ends up inside you twenty minutes after you show up on campus. I'm sorry, Owen, but I just can't think of anyone who might want me dead. If anything, I should be suspect number one if anything happens to Roger or Mary-Louise." She sees my expression, but misreads it and adds, "Kidding, kidding. Jesus, Owen, I'm not *that* crazy."

I smile, but the real reason for my expression drives away mirth. Maya might not know who wants her dead, but someone does. Of that I'm sure.

And I will find them and make sure they can never hurt her again.

9

Maya

Four months later we still have no idea why someone started the fire. Owen still believes it must be someone wanting to hurt me, but he grudgingly accepts there might be another possibility, one that might even include some kind of random attack by a crazy firebug who just chose my lab as some kind of a test or a first foray into serial arson.

The one thing we know for certain is that the fire is not accidental. There were millions of dollars of damage, mostly because of the lab equipment, but given the amount of money at the Foundation's disposal, there isn't any question about a monetary motive or an insurance motive. In fact, the Foundation is, if anything, underinsured at this location.

So, there's no progress at all for four months.

Let me amend that statement because right now, Owen is on the couch at my place and I'm on top of him. My hips roll over him and every movement seems to highlight the power of the sensations rocketing through my body as I kiss him. So, I guess it's fair to say that things continue to progress very well in that regard.

It's early in the morning. In general, we make love in the afternoon or evening with an occasional morning blowjob. We're all out this morning, though, because he'll have to return to the station for four days today. So, I wake him up with my mouth very early, drag him out here and proceed to screw him like crazy.

Yeah, I want him thinking about me all four days.

I'll be thinking about him. You can count on that.

I'm falling for him. Hell, maybe I already fell. He's not only attentive and sweet but he's also strong, distant, and stern. God, I can't explain it. I guess I can say it feels a lot like being girlfriend to a king. It's like there's distance between him and every other person, but I get to be close to him. I make that distance disappear.

And there's more about him that fascinates me from a scientific standpoint. His numbers are all off. He's the healthiest tiger I ever meet. Hell, he's the healthiest shifter I ever meet. He has strength that goes far beyond what he ought to have, stronger even than bear shifters, and I've seen bear shifters flip garbage trucks. He has an incredible internal rate of recovery from any exertion, and I've actually seen a scratch on him in the morning that heals by early afternoon.

If I can figure out what makes him so damned special physically, it can lead to medical miracles.

But right now, what matters to me are miracles that have nothing to do with medicine. "God! Owen!" I cry as I feel my climax rise to the edge. "Owen!"

When the orgasm hits, it feels like fireworks go off inside me. I shriek and scream and moan and yes, those are three different sounds, and I make them on repeat as I feel every inch of my pussy squeeze and twist and suck on his wonderful, glorious cock.

As usual, he's not satisfied with me cumming harder than medical science believes possible. He wants me to cum harder than anyone has ever conceived of in the past, so he slides his fingers down to make sure my clit cums just as hard as my pussy.

Then he leans over and suckles my nipple while I cum, and it basically feels like I have three phenomenally powerful orgasms at the same time and those orgasms combine to make a fourth orgasm that's so powerful I think with only a slight amount of sarcasm that if someone wants to kill me, paying Owen to make me cum like this will probably do the trick.

When I'm finished, he's filled my pussy twice because I'm so tight after the first time that he can't pull out of me without hurting me, so he has to stay inside me until my exhaustion finally overwhelms my pleasure.

We shower together, and I finally manage to get my mouth on him and take a third load of his on my face. I've taken him in my throat and my mouth before, and he's cum on my tits, but this is the first time anyone's cum on my face.

I like that.

When he leaves, I head to the lab. Oh yeah, the lab's back up and running, or rather the new lab the Foundation builds at a secret location. We have very wealthy and very powerful friends, like I tell Owen.

I run his numbers a few more times, looking for something, anything, that might tell me why Owen is such a god among gods. I mean, an average shifter is already close to superhuman compared to normal humans, but Owen is like the Hercules of shifters. It's impossible that he can be so utterly superior to every other living thing, but there it is, and I need to know why.

Anyway, I run his numbers again, and while I'm running them, I hear Chirp call my name.

"In the lab!" I call.

I hear footsteps, and when the door opens, I smile and turn to Chirp. My smile vanishes the instant I see her, or rather the instant I see the man standing behind her with his gun to her head.

I should have known. Goddammit, I should have known. Of course.

Owen asks me if there's anyone who might want to hurt me. He specifically asks if a former lover might want to kill me, and I laugh when he does, because Roger is so happy when Mary-Louise comes back, that I think she could die, and he wouldn't even think about me at all. Mary-Louise, if she's jealous at all, isn't jealous after Roger kisses her and gets his hand under her panties before remembering that he should probably break up with me before fucking his new-old girlfriend.

But Chirp. I never even think about Chirp.

God, I'm such an idiot. I suppose Owen is too. We both focus only on me because I'm the Xavier. I'm the heir to the Foundation. I'm the one with the money, the influence, the connections, everything anyone might want.

Unless what they want is to hurt Chirp.

Roger doesn't feel upset at all about losing me, and Mary-Louise doesn't begrudge me the few years I have with Roger, but Mark is devastated when Chirp breaks up with him, and even more upset when she responds to his threat to make sure no one else can ever have her by getting a restraining order and having her bodybuilder brother scare the shit out of him.

He smiles at me, and the crazed look in his eyes tells me there's no hope of reasoning with him. He intends to kill both of us, and nothing I can say or do will stop him.

For the second time in four months, I am going to die.

10

Maya

"Mark," I breathe out, "you don't want to do this."

I know that I can't convince him to stop, but maybe I can slow him down long enough for another miracle to arrive. Maybe Owen will show up and rescue me again. It's an impossibly long shot, I know, but I can hope. At the moment, that's all I can do.

Mark's eyes narrow a moment, and he says, "Not to you, I don't, but now there's no choice." He says bitterly, "See what you did, Willie? You hurt everyone around you, and now you've hurt Dr. Xavier, too."

"What do you hope to accomplish here, Mark?" I ask. "If you hurt Chirp, she's never going to be with you."

"Shut up!" he says. "I need to think! You ruin everything! All the time!"

I go over all the possible courses of action in my head. I don't have any. I take a breath and watch Mark. He's clearly unstable. He lifts a hand to his head and tangles his fingers in his hair. That's when I see straps and wires around his chest. He has a bomb. This is a suicide mission.

Chirp says, "I know I… I deserve this, Mark… but let Dr. Xavier go. She didn't hurt you. I did." I can't believe the bravery of this girl. I would protest, but that won't help save her.

He says, "It's just more hurt that you've done!" He pushes her toward me, and she stumbles against me. My heart beats crazily as I use the distraction to grab my phone. I have only a second and do the only thing I can think. I text Owen.

Help.

That's it. That's all I can do and only because the autofill finishes the word. I plan to turn that setting off because I'm tired of having fuck changed to duck and asking Owen to duck me, but thankfully I don't. I stand up under the guise of helping Chirp steady herself and set my phone back on the table while I do my best to keep Chirp between Mark and the sight of me doing that. "Mark, do you want us to stand here or to sit down?"

My phone rings, of course. I glance at it. It's Owen. "Let it go to voicemail!" Mark shouts.

"Okay," I say, "But it's a conference call. It will go to voicemail and then he'll call again. He'll keep calling because my signal isn't very good here and he'll assume that's the problem. You should let me get rid of him."

"Do it!" he says, "But don't do something stupid."

I answer with, "Hello, Owen. Thank you for calling. I'm afraid I can't do our conference call today."

"What the hell is going on?"

"Yes. I appreciate it. Chirp and I just have some unexpected work we need to do here so I have to reschedule."

"Who is it?"

"Yes. Let's try to get together as soon as possible," I say. "I need to go now." I turn the volume off and say, "There, I got rid of him." As I set the phone down, I see Owen is still listening. "How did you find out where the new lab is?"

"I'll always know where Willie is!" Mark shouts. "That's what you don't understand Willie. We belong together. You belong to me. You always ruin everything!"

I'm not sure if he's saying that to me or to Willie, but I know that Owen hears him, and since Owen and I christen the new lab in exactly the way you'd expect two people who really love ducking each other would, he knows where it is too.

Now we have a chance. I just need to keep him talking.

"Why are you doing this, Mark?" I ask. "You love her."

"That's exactly why I'm doing this!" he shouts. "I love her! She belongs to *me!* I gave her everything, and she left me so she could suck her neighbor's fucking shriveled old cock!"

Chirp's neighbor, Harold, is eighty-three, and if he even could get it up anymore, he's as gay as a summer sky. Chirp reminds him of this, "Mark, I didn't do anything with Harold! We were dancing because it was his fucking birthday and his partner—his partner *David,* had just died and he had no one to celebrate with!"

"Yeah, but I know what happened after," Mark says, apparently not registering that a man who spends fifty-eight years living with a man is probably not interested in anything a woman might have to offer him. "I saw you shaking your hips and thrusting your tits into his face! Just because I didn't stick around to watch doesn't mean that I don't know what went on!"

I see Chirp's eyes narrow in anger. Before I can signal her to stop before she antagonizes him further, she shouts, "Mark, for fuck's sake! *This* is why I broke up with you!

There was no other guy! There *still* is no other guy! I left you because of your bullshit, psycho jealousy!"

He strides toward her with his jaw clenched, and Chirp realizes her mistake. "But I was wrong!" she says quickly. "I was wrong. I should have apologized, and—and I shouldn't have seen Harold anymore. You were right. I belong to you, and I should never have seen anyone you didn't approve of!"

I see the intent in his eyes too late. I try to throw myself in between the two of them, but the barrel of the gun crashes onto Chirp's forehead before I make it. I grab his arm, but he throws me off easily, then points the gun at me. "I swear to fuck, I will kill you slowly if you try that again," he says.

The hand holding the gun shakes, but not enough that I feel confident I can avoid being shot, so I only lift a hand and say, "Okay, okay. Just please don't hurt her again."

His eyes widen in shock that would be comical if he wasn't about to kill both of us. "I would never hurt her!" he says, "I love her!"

So saying, he pulls the bleeding, groggy Chirp into his arms and kisses her deeply, shoving his tongue into her mouth, but keeping the gun steadily pointed at me. I hear Chirp weeping softly, and then a moment later, he pushes her away. She lands against the wall and sinks to the floor, weeping, and he says, "Why are you crying? We're going to die in each other's arms like we always wanted. Why are you crying? Why are you *crying!*"

He points the gun at her, and I get quickly to my feet, but he grabs her and lifts her by the throat, pointing the gun back at me before I can reach him.

"I'm going to kill you now," he says, and his voice is calm, almost casual. "Then Chirp and I are going to explode together."

I look at my phone, which still blinks. Owen is listening, and he won't make it in time. "I'm sorry, Owen," I say.

Mark frowns. "Owen? Who's—"

He never finishes that sentence. With a sudden crash, the hardened, blast-proof, steel-reinforced door shatters like glass and a giant tiger strides inside with a roar and with a swipe of one massive paw, sends Mark flying.

11

Owen

Maya shouts, "Owen!"

Chirp shouts, "Oh, my God!"

Mark screams an unintelligible scream and I see him reach for a handle attached to his vest. I realize at that moment that guns are the least of my worries. I don't know a lot about bombs, but I imagine if he pulls that lever, I'll be the only one getting out of this place. It's not even guaranteed I'll survive. Dragons are incredibly tough, but we're not invulnerable. Maybe back in the days of swords and spears it was next to impossible to kill us, but gunpowder changed all that. It's one of the primary reasons we don't reveal ourselves to humans. We can't risk being targeted by people with more fear than sense.

There may be some hope for the girls if I keep my body between them and this man. So, I just act. I leap forward.

In tiger form, I'm about three times the size of a normal tiger. Ordinary tiger shifters are about twice the size. My parents and I believe that my size comes from my dragon blood. I know it's an inappropriate time to think about such things, but I wonder what Maya will make of the sight of me. Chirp says, "Giant tiger!" and it occurs to me she has no idea what Maya actually does.

I rake my claws over the man's face because I don't know if doing that to the bomb will cause an explosion. It has the effect I want, and both of the man's hands immediately come up as he screams and covers his face with them. I swipe again from the other direction and this time hit him on the side of the head. He flies toward the door and lands in a crumpled heap there. I pad forward and check. He's down for the count. I turn around and shift.

Chirp says, "Holy shit." Her voice is a whisper, awed.

Maya simply runs forward and throws her arms around me. I hold her and over her shoulder I say to Chirp, "You're safe now."

Chirp says, "You're a shifter…. I knew they were real!" She shakes her head and says, "How did you… Oh my God."

Maya doesn't let go of me, but she says, "We're going to have a lot to talk about Chirp."

"Okay," she says.

She's utterly shellshocked, and I don't blame her. I look at Mark's prone form, and a growl rises in my throat. People like him shouldn't exist. They shouldn't be allowed to exist. They're blights on humanity, and they should be removed from the Earth.

Maya puts her hand on my cheek and turns me to face her. "It's over," she says. "Don't do anything you'll regret."

Perhaps it's my shifter's perspective, but I would feel absolutely no regret at tearing his throat out. Maya would, though. She might understand my choice, but she could never condone it. That fact alone saves Mark's life, although soon all three of us will realize what a mistake that decision is.

"All right," I say. "Come on. I'm going to take you outside and we're going to call the bomb squad. Maya, is there a way to seal the door in case he wakes up?"

I wonder sometimes if the rumored prescience of dragons really does have some basis in reality. It certainly seems that way right now. As soon as I say that, Chirp screams and points at Mark.

I stare in amazement as Mark, barely conscious and bleeding from his ears and nose, somehow manages to pull himself to his feet and lift the detonator in his hand.

His last words are words that I believe his crazed mind might actually believe are true, although his actions make it very clear that they aren't.

"I love you, Willie," he says.

Once more, I act instantly. I gather the women into my arms and leap into the air. In the air, I shift into dragon form and the building crumbles around me even before the blast of heat and pressure and the cacophonous boom that follows a split-second after tells me that Mark manages to set off the bomb.

I feel heat and shrapnel impact my scales, but fortunately, dragons turn out to be resilient enough to handle a glancing blow from a makeshift bomb vest and I am not injured. Maya and Chirp are wrapped safely in my talons and pressed against my chest, so they don't suffer any harm either.

We fly for about twenty minutes in silence. I debate keeping them covered for the entire flight, but in the end, I decide to let them see. The imagination is often more frightening than reality.

"Oh wow," Chirp says as soon as she sees the ground, which is now about fourteen thousand feet below us. I can fly much higher without discomfort, but humans have trouble breathing air any thinner than this, so I stay where I am while Chirp gawks at the ground and back at me.

Maya says nothing, but the awe in her expression as she regards me is enough for me to know that she's just as overwhelmed as Chirp is.

I don't blame them. My wings stretch over a hundred fifty feet from tip to tip, and my body is the size of a small whale. My scales are less showy than some dragons, but the burnished copper shines like the fire that I can generate but rarely do in the light of the afternoon sun.

"Oh my God!" Chirp exclaims. "Dragons are *real?*"

I can't smile in dragon form, at least not in any way a human could recognize, but I can't help but feel a touch of pride at the childish exuberance exhibits. At some point, I will have to tell her that she can't tell anyone else about me, but I'll save that for later. For now, I just let her enjoy herself.

We fly about two hundred miles and then I dive downward. Chirp shrieks in glee, and Maya's eyes are big as saucers as we descend toward a small circular clearing in the middle of the forest. At one end of that clearing is a small wooden cabin used by shifters who go running—that's one of the terms shifters use for shifting into animal form, although flying shifters like eagles use the less common term go wild, since shifting involves very little running for them. The cabin's remote location allows us to avoid the prying eyes of non-shifters.

I wonder if any dragon has been here before. I know of the cabin from my tiger form, but this is the first time I arrive as a dragon.

I worry the cabin might be in use, but I don't smell anyone else, and we land directly in front of the building.

"Oh wow," Chirp says again.

Maya only continues to stare.

I shift back and say to Maya, "And now, we have a lot to talk about."

12

Maya

"My God, he's got a big dick," Chirp says.

We're at a gas station. She and I are in the car and Owen is pumping gas. I shake my head and say with a laugh. "Really? That's what you're taking from this whole experience?"

She shrugs and says, "Well, I saw it for like an hour and a half straight."

"Still," I say, "Your crazy stalker tries to kill you twice and you're rescued by a tiger shifter who also turns out to be a dragon shifter—and that's impossible, by the way, or at least we thought so until now—and you're focused on the guy's penis?"

"It's a very impressive penis," Chirp says.

"Well, it's spoken for already, Chirp," I say.

"Oh my God! You and him? You're..."

The door opens and Owen gets into the driver's seat. I

have to admit that as silly as Chirp is being, I do kind of wish the Xavier Foundation wasn't so efficient. The landline in the cabin gets a call to my home base and that gets a car to us withing an hour of our arrival there along with clothes for Owen. I could have enjoyed another hour or so with him undressed.

God, now I'm thinking like she is.

At the cabin, I give Chirp the basic history of the foundation. I swear her to secrecy about the truth of the Xavier family and Owen swears her to secrecy about his dual animal nature. She agrees as long as he tells her if he can breathe fire. So, he takes us outside the cabin, shifts, and sends gouts of flame up into the air. Chirp giggles and claps her hand like a little girl, and I can't help but smile.

But now he's dressed and we're on the way home.

He's impossible. Dragons can only mate with humans. Well, I guess a dragon can fuck anyone he wants to fuck but they can't produce offspring with nonhumans. His mother is a tiger. That isn't possible. Set the whole dragon thing aside, it's not possible for a shifter to have two animals! When two shifters with different animals mate, the offspring are always one or the other, never both!

"What happens now?" Chirp asks.

"The city and the Xavier foundation sweep this under the rug," Owen says, "And a new lab is built—probably to the specifications of an underground nuclear bunker—and everyone pretends nothing happened."

"How can…"

"It won't be the first time," Owen says.

Chirp looks at me and I nod. "My family has been sweeping things that impact shifters under the rug since before your great grandmother was born," I say, "And this never happened."

Chirp looks down for a moment and then asks, "So will I be your real assistant now?"

"You mean doing shifter research?" She nods and I shake my head. "No."

I can see a tear in her eye. "Another thing Mark stole from me."

"No, Chirp," I say, "I'm going to see to it the foundation sends you to medical school so you can get your doctorate. You'll never be anyone's assistant again. We'll work together as equals."

She looks at me in shock. "You… you mean…"

"Yes," I say, "You're going to get your degree and then both of us will work together as partners. You'll have an assistant of your own, and everyone will call you Dr. Chirp."

"Or Dr. Willie," Owen suggests.

"Eww," Chirp says, wrinkling her nose. "Definitely not that."

"You'd be pretty damned popular with the boys if you were Dr. Willie," I say, "Imagine that." I put on a sultry voice and say, "Hello, boys. I'm Doctor Willie. I have exactly the right prescription for willies of every size and shape."

"Oh God!" Chirp says through giggles. "Stop!"

"Ooh," I moan, "What a big Willie you have. All the better to inject me with, right?"

"Stop!" Chirp shrieks, leaning over and covering my mouth.

Owen and I continue to tease her until we reach her house. When we drop her off, she kisses Owen on the cheek and says, "Thank you, Owen."

"Don't mention it," he says, "Any friend of Maya's is a friend of mine."

She releases him, and when he turns around, she points

in between his legs and nods in approval before giving me a thumbs up. I roll my eyes and chuckle as I follow Owen back to the car.

"What's so funny?" he asks.

"Nothing," I say.

"Is it because Chirp congratulated you on getting to use my big dick?" he says.

I stare at him and redden, and he laughs and says, "Dragons have incredible hearing. I heard you two talking earlier. Don't worry, I won't say anything to her. If it's all right with you, though, I might give my friend Lucas her number and suggest to him that she might appreciate a check-in late at night with a bottle of wine."

I remember the way Chirp looks at Lucas when he visits her in the hospital and say, "I think that's an excellent idea."

"Done," he says. "Although after seeing my dick, Lucas's might be a little bit of a letdown."

I shove him playfully, and he laughs. "It's a good thing you're not completely arrogant," I say, "Or you'd be *really* annoying."

"Hey," he says, "It's hard not to be arrogant when I rescue a girl from certain death and then head home with her to fuck her into a stupor."

I shiver as a thrill runs through me and say, "Who said we were gonna have sex?"

"I did," he said, "I'm also going to eat your pussy and finger you until you can't walk."

"Before or after you fuck me?" I ask.

"Yes," he says.

I shiver again and though it's only three minutes to cover the rest of the distance to my house, I spend it extremely impatient.

As soon as we arrive, our clothes come off. As I lay on

the bed and open my legs, I ask, "Tell me, Owen, can you set things on fire when you're not in dragon form?"

Spoiler alert: yes he can. God, yes he can.

EPILOGUE: ONE YEAR LATER

Maya

"Well," I say, "you're still a mystery."

Owen smiles and says, "Chicks dig a mysterious man. I can live with that."

I roll my eyes but the truth is, I like his silly joke. I like everything about him. "Well," I say, "I'll figure it out eventually. The real issue is that dragons are the shifters with the least data available. There aren't very many of them comparably and the lifespan is so long... Well, I guess medical research for someone who just doesn't die isn't something that commands a lot of attention."

"Really," he says, "You care more about figuring this out than I do, Maya."

"I know," I say, "but since it's a mystery, I can't help myself."

"The real mystery we need to figure out is how the hell a kid so small can eat so much." He kisses my forehead and then caresses the back of Andrew's little head. I think

Andrew's suckling changes a little at my breast but that's probably just sentiment.

"Shifter babies always eat more," I say, "you should know that."

I know he's a shifter because shifters can immediately tell a shifter of their kind. Human and shifter pairings can either produce straight humans or shifters. The moment Andrew is born, Owen knows he's a shifter even though he won't actually shift until he's at least eight years old. Andrew is definitely a tiger. He may be a dragon. Owen's father couldn't tell he was also a dragon until later, at around four years old. So, there's no telling about that. It will be interesting if Andrew is a dragon is because Owen is already a huge anomaly. Until him, it is believed Dragons can only produce offspring with human beings. There are no female dragons. Nobody knows if there ever were except there are legends and histories of natural dragons, non-shifters, who are female.

"Where did you just go?" Owen asks.

I smile and say, "I can't turn off my brain but I'm right here. I'm right here with you."

He smiles and kisses me gently. "And that's where you belong."

Damned straight it is. "I love you, Owen," I say. I don't think I'll ever get tired of saying that.

"I love you, too, Maya," he replies. I know for a fact I'll never get tired of that.

Did you like *Tiger's Deadly Secret?* I really enjoy writing (and reading, of course) shifter romance, and I love when I get a chance to write about shifters that don't necessarily fit into the typical shifter box. Don't get me wrong. I like the typical shifters. There's nothing like an alpha wolf, a warrior bear, or a haughty lion, right? Still, I just love looking at things from a different perspective and I love exploring new ideas like a shifter with two animals. I think I fell in love with Owen a little bit. I fall in love with all my leading men but Owen is sure to have a special place in my heart for a very long time, I think. Owen and his lovely lady are in for a wonderful happily ever after life, a life neither of them dared to hope they would have, a life that is certain to be filled with joy.

Wait until you see what's in store for the next sexy Company 417 fireman shifter to fall in love!

More than most lone wolves, Gray King likes solitude. Apart from his brothers, the firefighters at Company 417, he's not interested in friends. He's not interested in romance, either. He's fine with an occasional night of passion but the next morning, he's ready to get back to being what he wants to be, alone. That all changes one evening when he heads to a high-end bar on the top floor of a swanky hotel to see about a companion for the night. A devastating accident puts everyone in jeopardy and the girl he hoped to bring to his bed instead becomes the key to saving the patrons trapped in an inferno. With his brothers on the ground and Gray forty-eight stories above, Company 417 will have to work harder than ever before to keep tragedy at bay. As for this lone wolf, he's determined to make sure everyone makes it out alive. Looking at Marissa Taylor, though, he's not sure he can say the same about his desire for solitude. Can Gray and Marissa save the day? Will they discover something that burns hotter than the flames? Find out in *Lone Wolf's Raging Fire,* the next sexy and exciting tale in the always romantic and steamy *Company 417 Shifters* Series!

Printed in Great Britain
by Amazon